FINARIA
THE SAVAGE SEA SNAKE

With special thanks to Brandon Robshaw

www.seaquestbooks.co.uk

ORCHARD BOOKS
338 Euston Road, London NW1 3BH
Orchard Books Australia
Level 17/207 Kent St, Sydney, NSW 2000

A Paperback Original
First published in Great Britain in 2014

Sea Quest is a registered trademark of Beast Quest Limited
Series created by Beast Quest Limited, London

Text © Beast Quest Limited 2014
Cover and inside illustrations by Artful Doodlers,
with special thanks to Bob and Justin © Orchard Books 2014

A CIP catalogue record for this book is available from
the British Library.

ISBN 978 1 40832 857 6

1 3 5 7 9 10 8 6 4 2

Printed and bound by CPI Group (UK) Ltd, Croydon, CR0 4YY

Orchard Books is a division of Hachette Children's Books,
an Hachette UK company

www.hachette.co.uk

FINARIA
THE SAVAGE SEA SNAKE

SEA QUEST

THE PRIDE OF BLACKHEART

BY ADAM BLADE

ORCHARD

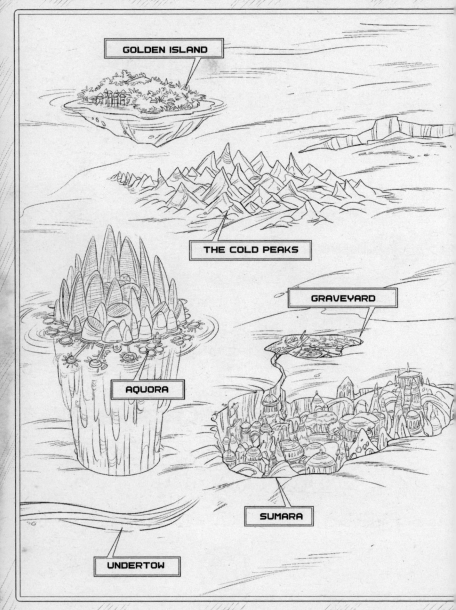

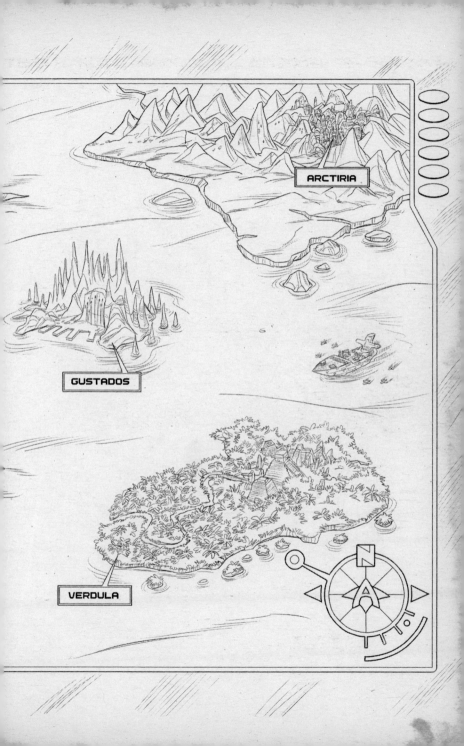

URGENT – PLEASE RESPOND

Mayday! Hostile vessels were detected at 1632 hours off the starboard bow. The Pride of Delta has now been boarded by pirates. I am not sure how long we have...

Be aware, the Kraken's Eye will soon be in the hands of the pirates. Please do whatever is necessary to secure the keys. The pirates must not be allowed to operate the weapon.

Rest assured I will not surrender the ship. We will remain in position until we receive a response, or until the ship is taken by force...

END

Message delivered: 1648 hours – Responses: 0

CHAPTER ONE

MEETING WITH A MONSTER

Max scanned the shelves that lined the ice walls of the cavern. Gadgets, electrical equipment and weapons were lined up, each one spotlit in a pool of yellow light. The people of Arctiria cared about beauty more than anything else, and although this cavern was only a place to store confiscated tech, it looked more like an art gallery. But Max wasn't bothered about how the place looked. Right now he had to find what he needed – and fast.

According to Jonah, the old keymaker they had met here in Arctiria, the pirates would be heading for the island of Gustados next. And Max had to get there before them!

I just hope Rivet brings reinforcements soon, he thought. His dogbot had gone to Aquora for help, but if the pirates – led by the terrifying Cora Blackheart, and aided by Max's uncle, the Professor – got to Gustados first, they could seize the key that activated the Kraken's Eye.

A weapon that could destroy whole cities.

"Hurry up!" Lia said, her teeth chattering through her Amphibio mask. "I'm freezing to death! And we need to get Spike back to the sea!" They'd left Spike in the main square of the city, being looked after by Arctirians. Lia seemed anxious to get back to her pet swordfish before the locals became too attached to him.

"OK, OK," Max said. "Wait a minute."

The pirate ship, the *Pride of Blackheart*, was

fast. Very fast. Max wouldn't be able to catch them up without increasing the speed of his aquabike. Which meant he needed to find a hyper-soldering iron... He moved along the shelves, picking up items and putting them down. He spotted a slender hyperblade, just like the one Cora took from him, and thrust it through his belt. Finally Max found the soldering iron he was after on a low shelf. He snatched it up. "Let's go!"

"At last," Lia grumbled. "Wasting our time rummaging through all this *technology*!"

Max didn't stop to argue. He and Lia left the cavern and set off as fast as they could, through the long, icy tunnels of Arctiria.

They came at last to the central square, in the middle of the ice mountain. Wreckage lay all around, from the recent battle with the ice lobster Robobeast, Nephro. There were shattered statues and fountains, shards of broken glass and chunks of masonry. A number of tall, blue, beautiful Arctirians were clearing up, stooping gracefully and putting the debris in silver bags. When they saw Max and Lia they scowled and turned away.

"What's the matter with them?" Lia asked.

"Still cross that their city got wrecked, I guess," Max said.

Spike was lying in the shallow pool where they'd left him. A pair of Arctirians kneeled beside him, sloshing water over him, murmuring and stroking him. At the sight of Lia, the swordfish lifted his bill in greeting.

"Don't worry, Spike, we're just about ready!" Lia said. "Give me a hand, Max."

Spike couldn't breathe out of water, so they needed to get him to the sea, fast. Between them they began to lift Spike out. The swordfish was heavy, slippery and very wet.

One of the Arctirians, a graceful, slender

woman with shimmering blue skin, tutted as Max and Lia took the swordfish away from her. "Why do you take this beautiful creature from its natural element?" she snapped. Her voice was as clear and pure as diamonds.

"His natural element is the sea!" Lia said. "Not in some fancy ice city. And I'm taking him back where he belongs."

"Why not leave him with us?" asked the Arctirian. "He's such a beautiful creature, he belongs among beautiful people, like us."

"*Hey*—" Lia began, but Max stopped her.

"It's no use arguing with them," he said. "Let's just take Spike and get out of here."

"Spike is coming with us!" Lia told the Arctirian. "And don't try and stop us, or there'll be trouble!"

The Arctirian held up her hands in horror. "Trouble is an ugly word. Take your fish, if you must." She sighed. "He is very beautiful."

"You got that right, at least," Lia said.

"And now," the Arctirian said, "we must get back to work – cleaning and repairing our lovely city, which you damaged in your battle with the ice lobster."

"So glad we were able to help," Max said, while Lia rolled her eyes. The truth was, they'd saved the city – and its people – from total destruction.

Carrying Spike between them, Max and Lia hurried towards the ice tunnel that led down to the waterfront. Some of the Arctirian people gave slow, languid waves as they passed. But Max heard one of them say: "I'll be glad when they've gone. I can hardly bear to look at the ugly little things!"

He saw Lia clench her jaw. "If we didn't have to get Spike back in water as quickly as possible—"

"Well, we do," Max said. "So let's get out of here!"

Jonah, the keymaker, was waiting for them at the edge of the water. He wore a long robe over his hunched shoulders and his white beard was flecked with ice crystals. The dark-blue sea slapped against the jetty of ice where Max's aquabike was moored.

Lia and Max immediately tipped Spike into the water, where he frolicked around happily, apparently unbothered by the cold.

"The pirates have departed for Gustados, to the south-west," Jonah said, pointing. "They have a lead on you, so you will need to hurry. Your aquabike is ready."

"Not quite!" Max said. He kneeled beside the bike and opened the engine casing. Using the hyper-soldering iron, he altered the engine settings, boosting the power. "There!" he said. "Last time I used the turbo, it nearly rammed us into the *Pride of Blackheart*. This time it should be a bit easier to control."

Lia was tapping her foot impatiently. "What are we waiting for?"

"Nothing," Max said. "Climb on!"

He sat astride the aquabike, and Lia got on behind him. Max attached his communicator headset, listening in for word from his father Callum, the Head Defence Engineer at Aquora. Spike swam up as Max pointed the aquabike to the south-west, revving the engine.

"Goodbye," Jonah said. "And be careful. Cora Blackheart is dangerous."

"I know," Max said.

He waved, then twisted the throttle. The engine roared as they tore away across the waves, so fast that even Spike had difficulty keeping up.

Lia still had her Amphibio mask on, so Max decided to stay on the surface for a while. It was good to feel the wind in his hair and the spray on his face. He had spent so much time underwater since he'd acquired his Merryn powers that he sometimes forgot what it was like to fill his lungs with air. *The Quest continues!* he thought, and felt excitement rise within him.

But a moment later he remembered his mother. They'd been separated since he was a little boy, and in Arctiria he thought he had found her again. But it had turned out to be an evil clone, not the real person herself – and Max had been forced to let the clone fall to its destruction off a cliff. Still, he held out hope that, somewhere, his mother was alive.

Lia suddenly tugged at his arm. "Look. That's the *Pride of Blackheart*, isn't it?"

Max saw the black bulk of the pirate ship up ahead. Sunlight glinted off its long metal sides, daubed with skulls. His heart beat faster. "We'd better dive," he said, "so we can overtake them without being seen."

"Great!" said Lia. "It'll be a relief to breathe pure water again."

Max grinned and tilted the handlebars forward, and the aquabike plunged beneath the waves. Spike dived down beside them,

and the world turned a deep bluey-green. Lia
pulled off her Amphibio mask and tucked it in
the bike's side pannier.

"Yesss!" Max said, his voice sounding more
Merryn underwater. He pumped his fist as
they passed the dark underside of the *Pride
of Blackheart*. The turbo-charged engine was
doing its job.

Suddenly, Max's headset crackled. "Max! Callum coming! With ships!"

"Hi, Rivet!" Max said, delighted to hear his robot pet's voice. The dogbot had succeeded – he was bringing Max's father and the Aquoran fleet to deal with the pirates. "Tell Dad to take the fleet to Gustados as fast as he can. We'll meet you there."

"Yes, Max! Rivet good?"

"Yes, Rivet. You're a good dogbot."

He snapped the communicator off again. "They're on their way," he told Lia. "But the pirates will get to Gustados before they do. We'll have to hold them off somehow, until my dad arrives with the fleet."

Lia nodded grimly.

The water was getting a little warmer as they left the *Pride of Blackheart* and the icy northern seas of Arctiria far behind. In the distance, Max saw a mass of dark rock rising up from the depths to the surface. "That must be Gustados," he said.

"Where?" Lia said, leaning over his shoulder. The water had suddenly became cloudy, full of swirling sand that stung Max's eyes and made him blink. A current seized the aquabike and tossed it up and down, jolting Max around.

"Oh no!" shouted Lia.

Max followed her pointing finger.

With horror, he saw a long dark form coiling through the water nearby. *A sea snake!* But a gigantic one, far bigger than any Max had ever seen before. Its body was purple, blotched with green, and its eyes, set in the sides of its head, were yellow. Metal spikes bristled around its neck and along its sides. *The Professor's latest Robobeast*, Max thought, with a lurching feeling in his stomach. *It has to be.*

The sea snake's huge mouth opened to display rows of curving, razor-sharp teeth.

CHAPTER TWO
CAPTURED

Max twisted the throttle. The engines roared and the aquabike leaped forward.

But the sea serpent was surprisingly fast. It shot in front of them at an unnatural speed, coiling its colossal spiked body in a vast wall and barring their way. Its giant head appeared out of the spiralling mass, turning towards them, razor-toothed mouth opened wide. *It's big enough to swallow the aquabike whole*, Max realised with a shiver of fear.

"Swim!" he yelled to Lia, preparing to

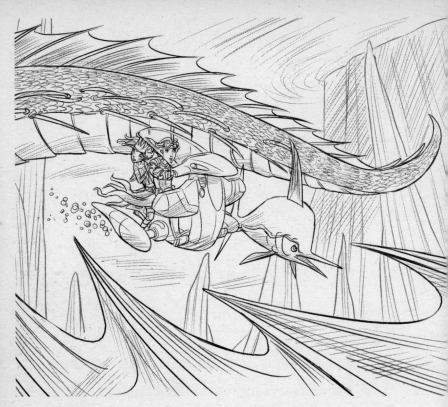

abandon the aquabike. Maybe the creature would go for the bike and leave them alone. Not much of a plan, but it looked like their only chance of escape.

Before they could move, however, there was a sudden, blinding flash, like a sheet of underwater lightning. But the light lingered, continuing to glow all around them, turning the water a luminous yellow. A moment later,

a strange sound surrounded them – like the long, unbroken chime of a bell. The noise was so unearthly, Max felt the hair at the back of his neck stand on end. The serpent froze, as if shocked by the sound.

"What is that?" Lia said uneasily.

"I don't know," Max said.

The light gave off a fierce heat. It seemed to have come from the island – the sea in the other direction was still dark. Spike gave a nervous whistle and moved closer to Lia.

Suddenly the sea serpent uncoiled and backed away, then streaked off into the darkness, tail whirling behind it like a propeller. It disappeared with unbelievable speed.

Definitely a Robobeast, Max thought. *No normal sea creature could move that fast.* He shuddered. He didn't want to meet that sea serpent again. But something told him he probably would…

"That was close!" Lia said. "What is that strange light, do you think?"

"I don't know," Max said. "Some sort of defence from the island – to scare off invaders?"

The glowing light was ebbing away, though the chiming continued. Max felt the water return to its normal temperature.

Lia patted Spike. "There, there, no need to be scared, it's gone now."

"Let's surface and see what's happening on that island," Max said. "This is getting weird."

"Going up, Spike!" Lia said, as she pulled her Amphibio mask on.

The sound got louder as they rose up. They broke the surface and Max saw an odd little ship coming over the shining sea towards them. It was sleek and metallic, painted in a riot of shimmering colours – red, green, orange, purple... It was clear that that was where the chiming noise was coming from. Spike dived back under the water, as though the noise was hurting his ears.

"What do you think?" Max said to Lia. "Go and check out the ship? Or get out of here?"

"Get out of here!" Lia said.

Max twisted the throttle and jerked the handlebars round. But before he'd completed half a turn, two long white tendrils shot out from cannons at the side of the ship and stuck

to the aquabike with soft *whump* sounds.
Alarmed, Max gunned the engine, but he
couldn't break clear. More tendrils shot out
from the ship and attached themselves to the
aquabike, entangling it more and more. The
ship turned and began to tow them towards
the island – a craggy pile of black rock in the

middle distance. No matter how much Max twisted the throttle, he couldn't break free.

"Well, we did want to go there!" he said at last. He touched one of the white strands. It looked foamy but felt strangely solid. And sticky. "This is weird stuff. Like rubber."

"Feels like the tentacles of an octopus," Lia said, frowning. "But it's not natural."

The island grew nearer. The ringing noise dwindled away as the ship slowed down, chugging into a harbour. The dock was built of smooth black stone at the foot of a steep, craggy cliff. Max couldn't see any settlement, only long ladders leading up to arched holes in the rock. He'd never seen a city like this before.

A hatch slid open at the side of the colourful ship, and two figures came onto the deck. They were human in shape, but they had pale, almost dead-looking white skin, their eyes were jet-black ovals set in their flat faces, and they wore light, silvery armour. Each one carried a blaster-like weapon.

Max waved at them. "Is this Gustados? We come in peace!"

The Gustadians didn't answer. They jumped up onto the dockside with an easy, fluid grace and motioned with their weapons for Max and Lia to follow.

Max scrambled up, followed by Lia. "Do you speak Aquoran?" he asked the humanoids.

"Or Merryn?" Lia said.

The strange people still didn't answer, but pulled on the tendrils that were attached to the aquabike and dragged it up onto the dock. *They must be incredibly strong*, Max thought. The aquabike was heavy, but the humanoids lifted it as if it were a toy. They dropped it on the dock with a clang.

"Hey, be careful!" Max said. "That's my bike."

He stepped forward and one of the

humanoids turned, pointing a weapon at him.

"Look out, Max!" Lia said. The other creature immediately pointed his weapon at her.

"You've got this all wrong," Max said, trying to speak calmly. "We're here to help you." He spread out his arms to show he was unarmed.

Instantly, the humanoid pulled the trigger. Sticky strands shot out and enveloped Max. It was the same stuff as before, only thinner strands of it. Max fought to break free, but the material hardened quickly, like glue drying. He couldn't move a muscle. The strange person tugged at Max and he fell to the ground, unable to get up or even struggle. He felt helpless – like a fly wrapped up in the web of a spider.

Out of the corner of his eye, Max saw more white strands shoot from the other Gustadian's weapon and hit Lia. Max was worried that her Amphibio mask would break if the sticky glue-like substance reached her face. Luckily

it remained intact, though she was dragged to the ground too.

"Spike!" Lia called out to her pet, who was still down in the water. "Swim away! But stay close to the island – we'll be back for you."

Max hoped she was right. Reluctantly, the swordfish flicked its tail and obeyed, disappearing below the surface.

He heard the sound of footsteps, and strained his neck to look up at the newcomer. It was another Gustadian, with the same pale skin and dark eyes as the first two. But this one wasn't dressed in armour. Instead he wore a long robe of shimmering colours and a strange, tall headdress that looked as if it was made out of seashells. A gold pendant hung around his neck.

He began to speak in a fast, fluid language that Max didn't recognise. After a few syllables, the gold pendant crackled and began to transmit his words, translated into Merryn.

"...General-in-Chief of Gustados. My name is Phero. You have approached our island without permission, accompanied by a dangerous monster which our defence system was fortunately able to drive away. You will live to regret your foolishness. You are now prisoners of war!"

CHAPTER THREE
PIRATE ATTACK

"Wait a minute!" Max said, in Merryn. "We didn't come to invade and we're not here to fight you. We came to help!"

"By bringing a monstrous sea serpent to our shores?" General Phero asked sarcastically. "We can do without that kind of help, thank you."

"We didn't bring it!" Lia shouted.

"Your people are in danger," Max said. "That sea serpent is under the control of a band of pirates. They're coming here now and they want to steal the key to the Kraken's Eye!"

General Phero started in surprise. All three Gustadians looked at each other.

"What do you know about the Kraken's Eye?" Phero demanded.

"We know that it's an incredibly powerful weapon that can't be operated without special keys – and you're guarding one of them here," Max said. "If you set us free, we can help you defend your island—"

Phero gave a short, sharp laugh. "Yes, that's a good idea. Two spies who know all about the key to the Kraken's Eye come to our island, with a giant serpent in tow, and I let them go free?"

"We're on your side!" Lia said. She pointed at Max. "He's Aquoran, and they're supposed to be your allies!"

"Aquoran?" Phero glared at Max. "I thought so. The Aquorans were once our allies, yes. But times change. Just a few days ago we arrested another Aquoran spy, sneaking around on our island. That's a funny coincidence, isn't it? He's in prison now. And that is where you are going, too."

"Who—" Max began. But Phero turned away and switched off his translator.

Max couldn't believe the Aquorans were really spying on Gustados. But he didn't have time to worry about it, because the Gustadians were moving towards his bike. They began to inspect it, talking in their own language. They were technologically advanced themselves, but Max guessed that they hadn't seen an aquabike before.

The General took a metal canister from his belt and sprayed something on the sticky tendrils covering the bike. Instantly the white stuff turned into blue foam and dissolved. Phero replaced the canister in the belt of his suit. Max felt suddenly hopeful. If they could get their hands on one of those canisters... He strained hard at his bonds, trying to get an arm free. But he still couldn't move a muscle.

"If only I could reach!" he muttered to Lia. He was sure that Phero couldn't understand him with the translator turned off. At least, he hoped not.

"Reach what?" Lia asked.

"The canister on his belt – but it's no use, we can't move!"

Lia grinned. "Can't we?" she said, and wiggled her fingers at Max, behind her back. One arm must have escaped the glue gun!

Phero returned to them and switched his translator on. "An interesting vehicle," he said. "We will learn much about Aquoran technology from it."

Out of the corner of his eye, Max saw Lia's hand snaking out towards Phero's belt. His heart was beating fast. He had to keep Phero talking.

"If you let us go," Max said, thinking hard, "you can have the bike."

The General laughed. "But I already have it!"

Lia's arm was at full stretch. Her fingers grazed the canister.

One of the Gustadians suddenly shouted out a warning as they rushed behind their leader.

General Phero stepped back, but he was too late. Lia snatched the canister, pointed it at Max and hit the button.

A cool blue mist enveloped Max, and he felt the strands holding him melt away, like snow turning to water. He leaped to his feet.

One of the Gustadians was already pointing a glue-gun at him. Max ducked underneath it, darted forward and knocked it from the Gustadian's hand. The weapon went clattering to the ground. Max dived, grabbed it, rolled and while still on his knees aimed it straight at the cluster of

Gustadians before him.

"Don't move, Phero. Or either of you other two." They might not understand Max's words, but the meaning was plain. The Gustadians stood still, watching to see what he would do next.

With his other hand, Max took the canister

from Lia's free hand and sprayed her with the antidote. The gluey tentacles turned to foam and fell away, and Lia jumped up.

"What do you hope to gain by this?" General Phero said. "You are alone on the island and outnumbered. You cannot defeat our whole population."

"I keep telling you, General, we're not here to fight you," said Max. "We're here to help!"

Suddenly there was a massive *BOOM!* like a crash of thunder.

Cannon fire.

Max heard the screech of a missile flying through the air above. A few seconds later, the dock shook violently beneath his feet and a chunk of rock from the cliff face came free, falling towards them. Narrowly missing the dock, it hit the sea with a great splash and sent up a fountain of water.

Clambering to his feet, Max stared out to the horizon. Sailing towards them was the familiar sleek, sinister shape of the *Pride of Blackheart*, with the skull and crossbones painted on its hull. He saw a silent flash of fire from the ship, and waited for the sound to reach them...*WHEE!* A whining noise started up, gradually growing louder. Horrified, Max saw a shape hurtling towards them through the air. "Get down!" he shouted, and threw himself flat.

There was an almighty *SMASH*. Max was soaked with spray.

He got shakily to his feet. A cloud of smoke rose from the surface of the sea. When it cleared, the Gustadian boat had gone. All that was left were a few brightly coloured pieces of it, floating on the water.

General Phero had gone even paler than before. "The Aquoran fleet has arrived!" he shouted. "It's war!"

"They're not the Aquorans, you idiot!" Lia shouted back. "That's the pirates!"

"No time to explain!" Max said. "They'll be launching that Robobeast again, Lia – let's go and get it!"

He and Lia pushed the aquabike back into the water, avoiding the splintered pieces of the sunken ship. The Gustadians seemed too taken aback to try to stop them. "Get the defence subs into action!" the General shouted at his men.

Max and Lia climbed onto the bike as a silvery sword cut through the surface nearby. It was Spike, swimming up to greet them.

"Hi, Spike," Lia said, patting his head. "Come with us. We must stop the pirates!"

They roared across the water towards the *Pride of Blackheart* as missiles zoomed

alarmingly close overhead.

A few moments later, long strands of the gluey tentacles went whistling in the other direction. Max looked behind and saw that cannons had appeared in gaps in the black, rocky cliff face of the island. *The Gustadians got their defences up and running pretty fast,* he thought. *But will it be enough?*

Missiles were landing all around them now, deafeningly loud. Plumes of water shot up in the air. Max and Lia raced through the smoke that had begun to gather over the ocean, trying not to choke on it.

"Safer down below, I think!" Max said. Lia nodded and tore off her Amphibio mask. They dived beneath the water, Spike hot on their tail.

It was quieter underwater. But not for long.

A powerful current took hold of the bike, almost turning it upside down. It could only mean one thing…

Max gripped the handlebars tight and looked around. The long, coiling, bristling shape of the sea serpent was racing in the direction of Gustados. And they were right in its path. At the last moment, Max jerked the bike out of the way of the beast. It went corkscrewing past, almost close enough to touch.

Max swerved to follow, but the creature was way too fast. Within seconds, Max was watching the Robobeast's tail-fins disappear through the murky sea. Even the turbo-charged aquabike couldn't keep up.

They saw the sea serpent about to head round the island. Max hit full throttle, following as best he could. He was just in time to see the long, wriggling shape of the sea serpent head for a dark underwater cave. It shot inside, as if it knew exactly where it was going.

"Now what?" Lia asked.

"We go after it, of course!" Max said.

"Agreed," said Lia grimly.

CHAPTER FOUR

FINARIA ON THE RAMPAGE

Max switched the aquabike's lights on, shining a powerful yellow beam ahead, as they entered the dark cave. The water had been churned into foam by the furious passage of the sea serpent, but there was no sign of it.

"That thing is fast!" Lia said.

Max nodded. "But it'll have to slow down if it's looking for the key. Maybe we can catch up before it finds it."

"And what's the plan then?" Lia asked.

"We'll think of something," said Max, trying to sound confident.

He twisted the throttle and the bike powered its way down the twisting tunnel. Soon the rocky floor began to rise, and the water became shallower. "Hang on," Max said to Lia. "We're about to surface."

Lia strapped on the Amphibio mask as Max brought the aquabike up into the air again. He heard splashing and shouts coming from around the next bend. "Something's going on!" he yelled over the roar of the engine, echoing through the tunnel.

They rounded the corner and came suddenly into a huge, brightly lit cave. *It must be the central part of the island city*, Max thought. Inside the cave the water was shallow and there were small islets sticking out, with stalls and shops. Long, glittering stalactites hung down from the roof, and stalagmites rose from the ground. Built into the sides of the cave were gleaming silver pods that Max guessed were the Gustadian people's homes.

But what really got his attention was the giant serpent coiling in and out of the islets at incredible speed, smashing stalactites as if they were twigs. Gustadian people were fleeing from the beast, splashing through the water or jumping into miniature subs and roaring away as fast as they could.

A group of Gustadian guards appeared on a walkway at the side and started firing glue-guns at the beast, the white tendrils smacking into the sea snake's body. It stopped dead. Max saw the muscles along its body ripple. Then, to his astonishment, the metal spikes that protruded from its side shot out like a volley of arrows, flying towards the Gustadians. The guards scattered – but one was hit by a spike

and fell into the water with a cry.

"That thing is deadly!" Max said.

"We have to do something!" Lia said. "But what?"

Max only had one idea. It was a big risk, but he couldn't think of any other way to save the Gustadians. He steered the aquabike straight in the direction of the serpent. Spike jumped up from the water, trying to stop him, but

there was no choice. Max accelerated towards the great Robobeast, quickly reaching top speed. He counted down the seconds until impact.

Three...

Two...

One...

He shut his eyes as the bike smashed into the serpent's side.

It was like crashing into a stone wall. The impact nearly knocked him and Lia clean off. The sea serpent let out an angry hiss and coiled round. Before they could fully recover from the shock, the serpent's giant head shot out towards them.

Time seemed to slow. Max saw the beast's purple and green face, the cold yellow eyes, the bristling collar of spikes and the black mouth with the curved, razor-sharp teeth. Bolted to its neck was a metal plaque engraved with the name FINARIA.

"Jump!" Lia shouted.

They dived into the water with a splash, just as the creature's jaws snapped shut above the bike with a terrible crunching sound.

A siren began to wail, and a voice echoed through the cavern. It was speaking Gustadian, but Max made out the name *General Phero*. The guards must be calling for his help.

Distracted, Finaria raised its head, giving Max and Lia time to swim back to the aquabike. Beneath them, one of the miniature subs raced past and the sea serpent took a sudden snap at it. Its powerful teeth ripped the metal sub wide open, and three Gustadian people fell into the water and began swimming for their lives. At once, the sea serpent was in pursuit, breaking off more stalactites as it plunged after them.

Maybe I can drive the Robobeast off with my hyperblade, Max thought. "Let's go!" he said to Lia. He revved up the engine and drove straight at Finaria again. This time, he turned side-on at the last moment and hacked at the creature with his hyperblade, while Spike jabbed at the serpent underwater with his sharp bill. The blows simply bounced off the creature's super-tough hide. But they were enough to attract its attention. Max swung the aquabike round and roared away through the vast cavern. Over his shoulder he saw the Robobeast chasing them down, bellowing out a sickening cry. Beyond, the Gustadians from the wrecked sub were clambering to safety.

Finaria was gaining fast. Its body rippled as it let loose another volley of flying spikes.

"Duck!" cried Max over the wailing siren. The deadly spikes whistled over their heads.

Some of the guards were firing their glue-guns from walkways high up in the cavern walls. Swivelling around, Finaria turned its attention on them, extending up and snapping at them. Nearby, Max noticed more guards regrouping on a walkway. He steered the aquabike towards them. "Maybe we can talk to the Gustadians and come up with some sort of battle plan together!" he said to Lia.

"Let's hope so!" Lia said.

Suddenly, Max saw General Phero running

along a walkway towards the guards, his long robe flying out behind him. He reached them just as Max and Lia climbed onto the walkway.

"You again!" General Phero said. "Guards, arrest them!"

"We're on your side!" Lia yelled in frustration. "We're fighting the monster!"

"It's true, General," said one of the guards. His words came out in Merryn through the General's translation device. "They've saved several of our people!"

The General looked at Max and Lia in surprise. "So you were telling the truth?"

"Listen, we don't have much time!" Max said. "You scared the sea serpent away with that light and the strange chiming noise when it first arrived. I think maybe it's sensitive to sound. Can you do it again?"

"Unfortunately not," said General Phero. "The Photosphere Noise and Heat Deterrent

was a prototype – the only ship that carried it
was destroyed by the pirates!"

Finaria was still rampaging around,
smashing pods and subs. Broken stalactites
and other bits of wreckage bobbed on the
churning water.

"We need to evacuate the area!" the General
said. "Get everyone to safety while we work

out how to fight that thing."

"Yes, but we have to make sure the key is safe before the pirates get here!" Max said. "Can you tell us where it is?"

The General hesitated, looking uncertain.

"They risked their lives to fight the monster!" one of the Gustadian guards said. "We should trust them, Sir."

The General looked Max in the eye. Max met his gaze. Then Phero gave a brisk nod. "Very well. You told the truth before. Just don't let us down now. The key is on the far side of the cavern. It is locked inside a square metal container, hidden behind a map of Gustados. There is a concealed button on the walkway, three paces to the left."

"Let's go!" said Lia.

Max jumped back onto his aquabike, and Lia leaped on behind him, Spike by their side in the water. The cavern was mostly empty now – Finaria was at its centre, nosing around among the wreckage, looking for Gustadians to eat. *We'd better not be next on the menu,* Max thought. Making his way towards the key, Max tried to steer as far away from the Robobeast as possible, hugging the side of the cavern.

In less than a minute they managed to reach the other side, without attracting the Robobeast's attention. Lia scrambled up onto the walkway, with Max close behind.

"There it is!" Lia said, pointing. The map of Gustados was etched on a square metal plate on the wall.

Max ran to it, quickly took three paces to the left, and stamped his foot.

With a high-pitched whine, the metal plate slowly swung open. Behind it was a compartment with a silver podium, on which stood a silver, flask-shaped container.

"The key must be in there!" Max said triumphantly, reaching out towards it. But suddenly his hand was cast in a shadow which grew up the wall in front of him.

"Look out!" Lia gasped.

Max spun round.

Looming over them was Finaria, its monstrous yellow eyes glaring, the spikes in its neck sliding out to their full length. But instead of striking out with its head, the serpent whipped its tail from behind, sending Max and Lia flying to the floor.

In an instant Finaria lunged forward, its jaws snapping shut over the silver container, before it slipped back, silently, into the water. Max couldn't believe it. The Robobeast had swallowed the flask whole – and with it, the key to the Kraken's Eye...

CHAPTER FIVE

LIA'S PLAN

"It's eaten the key!" Max said in disbelief, his voice echoing off the polished rock.

"Are you sure?" asked Lia.

"Positive," said Max. "General Phero said it was inside that container. And now it's gone."

The cavern was eerily quiet. Apart from a few guards, the Gustadians had all escaped. Max scanned the water for some sign of the Robobeast that was slinking beneath the surface. But he couldn't see it. "So what do we do now?" Max asked.

"Move, before it eats us too!" Lia shouted.

She caught Max's arm and pulled him aside, just as the Robobeast's massive head lunged up onto the walkway again. It missed Max by a hand's breadth.

"Thanks," gasped Max.

Max and Lia retreated to the far end of the walkway. Drawing his hyperblade, Max tried to keep sight of the sea serpent. Occasionally, he spotted it tracking them, swimming alongside as if making ready for another attack. There was no one else left for the Robobeast to eat.

"What's the plan?" Lia said.

"We have to somehow get the k—"

There was a blur of movement as the sea serpent shot out of the water. Max threw himself flat, swinging his hyperblade above him. The creature's jaws clashed shut, so close above him he could smell its briny breath. It gave a howl as Max's blade caught it on its scaly snout.

Max rolled and stood up, pressing himself against the rocky wall so that he was as far away from Finaria as possible. But it wasn't far enough. The sea serpent coiled round in the water, its yellow eyes fixed on him. It looked angry...

"Maybe we should get out of here," Lia said. "The Gustadians have all gone, and that Robobeast is deadly."

"But we can't!" Max said. "If it swims away with the key inside it we'll never get it back. If only we could make it cough the key up..."

"I have an idea!" Lia said. "Those glue-guns we took, they're still on the aquabike, right?"

"That's no good," Max said. "The Gustadians tried with the glue-guns and they didn't work."

"They were shooting from a distance," Lia said. "And we'll do it from close by. Just keep the monster busy, will you?"

Before Max could stop her, she dived into the water and swam off at top speed.

Finaria's head turned towards Lia. Quickly, Max struck his hyperblade against the wall with a clang. "Come on, Finaria!" he shouted. "I have something for you!"

The creature's tongue flicked out hungrily as it turned back to face him. Max tensed, getting ready for it to lunge again.

Without warning, Finaria let loose one of its spikes. It shot straight at Max like an arrow. He tried to dodge to the side, but was not quick enough. The metal spike pierced the side of his suit, grazing his skin and pinning the material against the wall.

Max tried desperately to pull free. But the spike was buried deep in the wall and there was no way he could dislodge it.

Finaria watched him. Its mouth opened. *It's got me just where it wants me, Max thought. And it's going to come back—*

Summoning up all the strength he possessed, Max tried to hurl himself to one

side. He felt himself being tugged back by the fabric of the wetsuit – saw Finaria's head rising from the water again in a blur of speed. This was it. He was going to be swallowed alive.

With one last effort, Max slashed at his suit with his hyperblade. The fabric parted and he stumbled to one side. He was free! He threw himself down, just in time. The creature's jaws slammed into the wall above, missing Max by a whisker.

It was getting closer each time. *Lia's still out there. How much longer can I keep this up?*

Max got up, panting, his heart thumping. There was a huge tear in his suit. He felt his side and winced with pain. His fingers came away sticky with blood.

Gripping his hyperblade, he faced the Robobeast. "Try that again and you'll get this right between the eyes – understand?" he shouted defiantly.

The Robobeast twisted its neck and fired off another spike. But this time Max was ready. He slashed at the missile with his hyperblade, knocking it away. It clattered harmlessly onto the walkway and fell into the water.

"Careful!" Lia said as she climbed out of the water. "That nearly hit me!"

She was holding the two glue-guns. She thrust one at Max.

"We have to get up close!" Lia said. "We can't let that sea snake get away with the key."

Together they stood right at the edge of the walkway, staring into the Robobeast's great yellow eyes. "Come on, Finaria," Max said softly. "Come and get us."

The creature stirred and coiled in the water.

Then it launched itself towards them.

Instantly Max pulled the trigger. A white, sticky tendril flew out and hit Finaria in the face. He saw another tendril shoot from Lia's glue-gun and stick to the creature's neck. The serpent flinched, pulling back from the attack.

Every instinct in Max's body was screaming for him to run as the monster hurtled towards him again. But he forced himself to stand his ground, Lia by his side, keeping his finger clamped on the trigger. They fired over and over again, and the sticky glue piled up around Finaria's head, neck and upper body.

The Robobeast began to slow. Its front half was completely covered now, like a fly wrapped up in spider silk. Moving its body closer, it tried to narrow the gap it would need to strike. Its head nosed onto the walkway.

Max and Lia held their nerve and kept firing, again and again.

The sticky glue hardened. *Nearly there*, thought Max. *Nearly...*

Finaria stopped dead. Its front half was now immobile, while its tail twitched feebly in the water. The Beast's glue-encrusted face was so close to Max that he could have touched it without straightening his arm. Its jaws were frozen, half-open. Strands of the sticky glue clung to its teeth. Max could feel its hot breath against his skin.

Max let out a long, shaky sigh. "OK. So far, so good," he said. "Now what?"

"Now," Lia said, "you just have to put your hand into its mouth and tickle the back of its throat. Then it will cough the key up."

"*Bleeurchh!*" said Max. "Why does it have to be me?"

"It's my plan. My rules," Lia said, grinning.

"Oh, really?" Max said. Still, someone had to do it. "Here goes, then."

Cautiously, he put his hand in between those curved, razor-sharp teeth. Finaria's jaws trembled – it was clearly struggling to break through the hardened glue and snap down. If it succeeded, it would take off Max's arm in an instant.

"Look out!" Lia screamed.

Max jumped back just in time. Finaria's huge tail came arching over, and whipped down onto its own head. The force of the blow smashed the glue crust and fragments went flying all over the cavern.

The sea serpent shook its head, giving a throaty bellow. It hauled itself up onto the walkway and slithered towards Max.

Max backed away. But the walkway soon came to an end. He was trapped – his back against the rocky wall, Finaria's monstrous form filling his field of vision.

"Spike!" Lia shouted. "Attack!"

Max heard a flurry in the water. Spike must be attacking the Robobeast, jabbing it with his sword. But this time Finaria wasn't going to be distracted.

Its mouth opened. The cruel teeth glinted.

This time, Max thought, *there's no escape.*

CHAPTER SIX

SNAKE CHARMING

Finaria slithered even closer. Max saw the saliva dripping from its teeth and smelled its fishy breath.

He lifted his hyperblade. If he had to die, at least he would go down fighting.

"NO! NO BITE MAX!"

Max started as a familiar electronic voice echoed around the cavern. It was Rivet, his dogbot!

From somewhere behind the sea serpent,

Rivet began to bark furiously. Finaria looked startled. Its spikes rose and its eyes widened. In that moment, Max acted.

He couldn't move sideways or backwards. There was only one way to go.

Straight ahead.

Max leaped forward and up.

Finaria snapped. The razor-sharp teeth

grazed the loose threads of his torn suit, but Max landed on top of the creature's snout, and jumped from there to the top of its head. *Don't think about what you're doing*, he told himself. *Just do it!*

Fixed to the snake's skull was a square metal box that Max hadn't noticed before, with cables running into the snake's flesh. *It's that box that's controlling the Robobeast*, Max realised. If he could somehow disable it... Then he spotted a camera lens set into the box, like an unblinking eye. *I bet the Professor's looking through that*, Max thought. *He must have fitted it so he could guide the Beast to the key.*

Max glared into the lens. "Hello, Uncle," he said, and raised his hyperblade to strike. Finaria bucked and writhed. Max tried to keep his balance, but he toppled over and slid from its head, falling into the water.

Before Finaria could twist around to get him, he swam under the serpent's body and headed as fast as he could towards the sound of Rivet's voice.

He surfaced to see Rivet paddling towards him, his red snout-light gleaming.

Behind Rivet came a tall man on an aquabike, dressed in the black and silver uniform of the Aquoran Defence Force.

"Dad!" Max shouted. His heart leaped for joy.

"Max OK? Max not eaten?" Rivet said.

"Max! Am I glad to see you!" Callum said.

Max pulled himself onto the aquabike. He hugged his father fiercely.

"Are you all right?" Callum asked.

"Just about," Max said. "Thanks to Rivet!"

Lia and Spike came swimming up. Spike and Rivet bumped noses in greeting.

"Thank Thallos you're OK!" said Lia.

"Yes – but we've still got to deal with Finaria!" said Max. He pointed across the cavern at the Robobeast. Its head rose high out of the water, the metal box on its skull still intact. It searched around until it spotted Max, Callum and Lia. Then slowly, menacingly, it began to move towards them.

"It doesn't give up easily, does it?" Lia said.

"I think the Professor is watching us

through a camera on its head," Max said. "He must be guiding it – trying to take us out, even though his Robobeast has already got the key for him."

At that moment, Max heard a strange, bell-like chiming, a bit like the sound he and Lia had heard from the first Gustadian craft they had met out at sea, but lower and more rhythmic.

Immediately, Finaria slowed down. Then it stopped, its long neck stretching out of the water, its head cocked to one side, as if listening.

Max looked around for the source of the noise. One of the Gustadian subs came gliding down the tunnel, seemingly looking for stragglers.

"It likes the noise!" Lia said.

The sub passed by and disappeared down an exit tunnel.

"It must be their engines making that sound," said Max. "Gustadian technology is really different from Aquoran. Maybe it's disrupting the Professor's robotics."

Now he was sure of it. Finaria must be sensitive to sound. He could have sworn that the Robobeast even looked a little disappointed as the noise from the sub faded away. It had seemed to be charmed by it. *Charmed...* An idea formed in Max's head.

"Do you have any music on you, Dad?" he asked.

"Sure!" Callum said. "I have some music programmed on my communicator." He pulled out a slender silver device. "If we could run this through Rivet's speakers..."

Max grinned. It was good to be back with his technologically-minded dad again. Very few of the people he'd met in the undersea world of Nemos really cared about technology.

"You'll have to be quick!" Lia said.

Finaria was moving towards them – not at top speed, but a steady pace, as if determined not to make any mistakes this time.

"We just need a little bit of time," Max said.

"All right. I'll distract it," Lia said. "Back to work! Come on, Spike!"

She jumped onto the swordfish's back and they raced across the water, straight towards the Robobeast.

"What music's on there, Dad?" Max said. "Got any *Psychotic Sharks*?"

"None of that rubbish!" Callum said. "What about Spilzen's *Third Symphony*, performed by the Aquoran Philharmonic Orchestra?"

"That might work," Max said. Normally

he didn't think much of his dad's taste in music, but something classical might be just the thing to calm the sea serpent down.

"Hold still, Rivet," Max said.

"Yes, Max. Rivet still."

Lia and Spike were close to Finaria now. Max saw it stiffen, then fire out a hail of spikes at them. They dodged in different

directions and the missiles shot between them. Max knew he had to work fast – it was only a matter of time before Lia's luck ran out.

With shaking fingers, Max unscrewed the control panel on Rivet's back. He found the dial for tuning the dogbot's wireless connection.

Finaria was streaking across the cavern now, in pursuit of Lia and Spike. The sea serpent was faster than the swordfish, but Spike was more mobile. Constantly zigzagging, he was just able to stay clear of the hungry jaws. But he was starting to slow down – it was clear Spike couldn't keep it up for much longer.

Here goes, Max thought. He turned the dial, smoothly and carefully. Suddenly, the tuneful sound of violins came wafting out of the speakers in Rivet's ears.

Finaria stopped dead still, listening intently, as if in a trance.

Spike and Lia curved round and started to swim back towards them, as Max let out a long sigh of relief.

"I think we've charmed it," Callum said. "What next?"

"First, I want to take out that robotic unit on its head," Max explained. "So that it's not under the Professor's control any more. After that, if it stays in its trance, we'll have to find a way to get the key out of its belly."

He swam over to the swaying sea serpent, wary in case it snapped out of its trance. Quickly, he clambered up to its head, using the spikes protruding from its side as foot- and handholds. Luckily, the creature didn't seem to notice him.

Max kneeled before the camera.

"Can you hear me through this, Professor?"

Max asked. "Just to let you know, you're about to get cut off!"

He raised his hyperblade, and struck down ferociously at the camera. The casing was made of steel, but it was no match for Max's vernium hyperblade. With a couple of blows the camera was in pieces, floating in the water below. Max waved to his father and Lia. He felt almost relaxed, as the strings of the concerto rose in one final flourish. Then it came to an abrupt stop…

Max felt the sea serpent shake itself beneath his feet, as if waking from a dream.

There was no time to climb back down. There was only one thing for it. Max swung his hyperblade hard at the cables that ran from the metal box into Finaria's skull. He felt them split under his blade, but he couldn't hang around to see what would happen next. He jumped off the Beast's head, sliding down its scaly body and splashing into the water.

As Max surfaced he saw Callum zooming towards him on his aquabike with Rivet swimming alongside, and Lia riding on the back of Spike.

"Fantastic job, Max!" his dad said. "Look!"

Max turned to see that Finaria was shaking itself like a dog. The metal spikes fell away first. Then the metal control unit went plunging down into the sea. In seconds the sea serpent had sent all the Professor's robotics crashing into the water. Finaria was free!

Max punched the air. "Yes! Now all we need to do is get that Beast to cough up the key, and then—"

There was a great splash as the sea serpent lowered its head into the water and began to swim away.

"No!" Max shouted. "We have to stop it!"

But the Beast was much too fast. It streaked towards the tunnel and disappeared, heading for the open sea.

"Oh, great!" Max said. Despairing, he put his head in his hands.

"What's the matter?" Callum asked.

"The key," Max said. "It's still got the key to the Kraken's Eye inside it!"

CHAPTER SEVEN
A SEA BATTLE

"We have to follow it!" Callum said.

"I don't think we'll catch it, Dad," Max said. "You've seen how it moves. It's faster than an aquabike!"

"The Aquoran fleet is outside, waiting to attack the pirates," Callum said. "I think one of our light battle-cruisers should be fast enough."

He took out his communicator and flipped it open. "This is Chief Officer North to Captain Henshaw. I want all men on the lookout for a sea serpent – if spotted, give chase immediately! Do you read me?"

"Did you say a sea serpent, sir?"

"Yes – a great big long thing, purple with green patches. You can't miss it!"

"Yes, sir. I— Wait, we're under attack!"

There was a crackle and the line went dead.

Callum looked fearful. "We need to go and see what's going on!" he said to Max and Lia.

Max had a bad feeling as he swam over to his own aquabike and climbed on. As fast as they could, they roared through the central cavern and back down the entrance tunnel, Max and Callum on their aquabikes and Lia astride Spike. Rivet wasn't able to keep up, so he rode on the bike behind Max.

As they neared the end of the tunnel, Max heard noises: the boom of missile launchers, the fizz of blasters and the hiss of Gustadian glue-guns. What was going on? Were the pirates attacking again?

They came out into the bay and Max saw at once that a massive naval battle was raging. It would have been an awesome sight if it hadn't been so scary. There must have been at least a hundred vessels involved, all gleaming in the bright sunlight. Gustadian ships and subs were firing giant glue-guns at the Aquoran fleet. The Aquorans were firing back with blasters and cannons. Some of the Aquoran ships were covered in the sticky tentacles, helpless and immobilised. A few of the Gustadian ships had been hit – Max saw several listing badly, and one was in flames.

"What's going on?" Callum said angrily.

The *Pride of Blackheart* floated some distance away, staying out of the battle. *Cora and her crew must be laughing*, Max thought, *seeing their enemies fighting each other!*

All of a sudden he spotted a long purple

and green shape streaking through the water, away from the battle, out into open sea. Finaria was free – that was one good thing – but now the third key to the Kraken's Eye might be lost forever.

Still, the pirates had no chance of tracking down such a fast beast. And that meant there was only one city remaining where they could get hold of a key.

Aquora.

Max gasped in shock as the realisation hit him. *Aquora – that's where the pirates will be going next!* Sure enough, a moment later he saw the *Pride of Blackheart* turning slowly in the water and heading south-west – the direction of his home city.

"Look, Dad!" Max said, pointing. "The pirates are going to Aquora! We need to follow them and defend the city."

"I'm afraid you might be right," said Callum

grimly. He flipped open his communicator
again. "Captain Henshaw – do you read me?"

"Yes, sir. We are attacking the Gustadian
fleet!"

"Then stop attacking them!" Callum
barked. "They're supposed to be our allies!"

"Aye aye, sir."

Moments later, the Aquoran fleet stopped
firing, and the ships that could still move

began to retreat. A mighty cheer went up from the Gustadian vessels. Obviously they thought they had fought off the invaders.

"Captain Henshaw!" Callum said. "I'll be coming aboard. We're going after the pirate ship. Cora Blackheart stole it from us, and we're going to take it back." Max's father turned to him. "This is going to be dangerous," he said. "The pirates are likely to resist, and that ship is extremely well armed. I know, because I helped design it. You'd better stay here."

"Come on, Dad!" Max said. He didn't want to be left out. "So what if it's dangerous? I've already fought a sea serpent today—"

"All the more reason not to run any more risks," Callum said. "You wait here."

When he spoke in that tone of voice, Max knew there was no arguing with him.

Callum swerved the aquabike around and

headed off for the Aquoran flagship.

"Bye bye, Max dad!" barked Rivet.

Max sighed. He felt frustrated and powerless to help. "Now what do we do?" he asked.

"There's General Phero!" Lia said. Max followed her pointing finger and saw the General, with two of his lieutenants, standing on the edge of the Gustadian dock. "Let's go and tell him what's happening."

"That's a good idea," Max said. "We can set the record straight."

General Phero eyed them suspiciously as they approached. "What do you want?" he asked haughtily.

"We've come to explain," Max said. He and Lia climbed up onto the dock to face the General. "There was no need to fight the Aquoran fleet—"

"There was every need," the General

interrupted. "They destroyed five of my ships!"

"Yes, but only because they were defending themselves," Max said.

"They came to help!" Lia said. "To protect the key from the pirates."

"That's a likely story!" General Phero said. "You've already saved the key, haven't you?"

Max opened his mouth, then shut it again. This didn't seem like a good time to explain that he didn't have the key at all, and instead it was in the belly of a sea serpent, heading who-knew-where.

"And how do you explain the spy?" one of the other Gustadians demanded. "If you Aquorans mean no harm, why did you send a spy to our island?"

Max looked at Lia, puzzled. He had forgotten about the spy. Who could it be? "Can we see this spy?" he asked. "Ask him some questions? I'm sure there'll be an explanation."

There was a pause. Phero stroked his chin and narrowed his eyes.

"Listen to me, General!" Lia said. Max looked at her in surprise. She was speaking in her proudest, most commanding voice – the voice of someone used to being obeyed. Max forgot, sometimes, that back in her own city she was a princess. "We have come here at great personal risk to ourselves. We have saved several of your people's lives and we have kept your key safe for you. You will now lead us to the prisoner so we can find out what is going on!"

The General blinked. He cleared his throat. "Very well," he said at last. "I suppose you have earned that right. I will take you to the spy."

"Well done, Lia," said Max in a low voice.

General Phero and the two Gustadian lieutenants led Max and Lia through an opening in the cliff face and down a long, twisting passage. It was lit by lamps along the walls, which shone with a strange green glow. The passage led downwards, and Max noticed the air getting colder as they descended. He just wished the Gustadians would move faster – he didn't like the thought of his father going after the pirates without him, even backed up by the whole Aquoran fleet. And what if the pirates reached Aquora first? Still, Max had a funny feeling that they needed to find out who this spy was.

At last, when they must have been deep underground, the General stopped before a thick metal door with a barred window.

"Spy? Where are you?"

A pale face with a black eye patch stared

through the bars at them. He looked strangely familiar.

It can't be, Max thought, *but it looks like...*

The face's single eye lit up in recognition. "Ahoy there, shipmates!"

"Roger!" gasped Lia.

CHAPTER EIGHT

A GENTLEMAN OF FORTUNE

"Roger?" echoed Max.

"Shiver me timbers, 'tis good to see you two again!" said Roger.

General Phero took an instrument from his belt which looked like a silver pen. He touched one end and it made a low humming sound, until the cell door clicked open.

Roger stepped out. He was thin and unshaven, but grinned at the sight of Max and Lia. "Good old Max, and Lia, the prettiest little Merryn girl in all the Seven Seas!"

"Oh, be quiet," Lia said, but Max noticed that she looked pleased.

"Come and give old Roger a hug!" said the pirate, putting one arm around Lia and the other – the one with the hook – around Max.

General Phero was watching them

suspiciously. "So you know this Aquoran spy?"

"Oh, old Roger ain't no spy!" the pirate said. "I've explained that about seven hundred times already."

"He's not Aquoran, either," Max said. "Who told you he was?"

"He did," the General said.

"The Gustadians caught me snooping around where I wasn't wanted," Roger said. "And I reckoned if I said I was from Aquora, the Aquorans would come and rescue me. But they never came."

"But what have you been doing, Roger?" Max asked.

"A bit of this, bit of that," Roger said. He shifted, and something clanked inside his clothes. "After I left you in the Cavern of Ghosts, I went adventuring. Came to Gustados just a few days ago and, like I say,

I was just sniffing around when these kindly fellows offered to put me up free of charge."

"Spying," said General Phero angrily. "That's what he was doing."

"What was that clanking noise?" asked Max.

"Just a few bits I picked up on me travels!" Roger said. He delved into his wetsuit and pulled out a small portrait of a Gustadian woman in a long robe with a crown on her head.

"That's Queen Higra the Thirteenth!" General Phero said. "How dare you?"

"Arr, and a fine-looking woman she is too!" Roger said.

"What else have you got?" Lia asked.

Roger unzipped his wetsuit a little further, and took out a chain of heavy gold links, a coral necklace and a sharkskin wallet.

"I don't understand," General Phero said.

"Why would a spy steal these things?"

"I ain't no spy!" Roger protested.

"He's a pirate," Lia said. "And it's just a sort of habit he has."

"He's not a danger to anyone," Max said. "He only takes small things and he always gives them back if you make him. He's just a bit of a nuisance, that's all."

Roger drew himself up, looking offended. "A nuisance, am I?" he said. "Only take small things? I've taken some pretty special items in my time as a gentleman of fortune, let me tell you!" He unzipped his wetsuit all the way, revealing a pair of underpants decorated with skulls and crossbones.

"What are you doing?" hissed Max.

"Stop it, Roger!" Lia said, turning away.

Roger reached into his underpants and brought out a glinting metal object.

General Phero's jaw dropped. "The key to

the Kraken's Eye!" he said.

"What?" Max and Lia said together.

Roger grinned, pleased with himself. "Arr, didn't expect that, did you? I knew this must be something pretty special, the way it was protected. Found it by accident one night before they caught me, while I was admiring a map of this fine city. It slid aside, see, and there was this little silver container in a secret compartment inside. Well, I took the key and left the container there, so no one would be any the wiser. I never did find out what the key was for, mind you."

General Phero took the key from Roger and turned to Max and Lia. He looked confused. "But – I don't understand. I thought you had the key."

"Oh, yes, we did," Max said, thinking fast. "Only when we hugged Roger just now, I slipped it to him and he hid it. All that stuff he said just now, that was just a joke."

Roger looked puzzled and opened his mouth. Lia quickly kicked him on the ankle.

"Ow!" Roger said. "What did you kick me for?"

"I didn't," Lia said.

"Well, who did, then?" Roger said, looking

around in bewilderment.

The General stroked his chin. "You Aquorans have strange customs," he said. "So – this man is on your side?"

"That's right," Max said. "We're working together. So if you could release him now, that would be a big help."

"Very well," the General said. "This man can go free. But I will hold you responsible for his actions."

"Wonderful," Roger said. "Thanks, shipmates!"

"Trust us on one more thing," Max said. "Cora Blackheart will stop at nothing to get her hands on a key, and she's heading for Aquora right now. That's where the last key is kept. She'll use the Kraken's Eye on every city in the Delta Quadrant. The Aquorans have gone to fight her, and we're going too. Will you help us?"

The General sighed. "If this is true, then we have no choice. The pirates must be stopped. Battle stations!"

Max felt a rush of excitement. At last there was going to be a showdown with Cora Blackheart and the Professor!

CHAPTER NINE

BRING IT ON

Max, Roger and Lia sat on a jetty, waiting for the Gustadian fleet to set out. Rivet sat beside them, his metal tongue hanging out, while Max's aquabike bobbed in the glittering water and Spike swam around beside it.

The Gustadian ships were being rearmed and refuelled in the harbour. Somewhere in the distance must be the *Pride of Blackheart* – almost certainly heading for Aquora – and Max was keen to get going. He wondered if

the pirates knew yet that two fleets were hot on their heels. Would they surrender? Or fight?

He thought of Finaria and smiled.

"What's funny?" asked Lia.

"I was just thinking of that sea serpent swimming around in the wild with an empty container in its belly," Max said. "I'm sure it'll cough it up eventually. Another one of the Professor's Robobeasts set free... That's something to be proud of, isn't it?"

Lia chuckled. "Yes, I don't think Cora will be too pleased about that!"

"Who?" Roger said suddenly, looking at Max. His face was pale and anxious.

"Captain Blackheart, the leader of the pirates," Max said. "Why, do you know her?"

"Of course he knows her," Lia said. "They're both pirates, aren't they?"

"There's pirates and pirates," Roger said, shaking his head. He looked serious. "She's the sort that gives pirates a bad name."

"Tell us about her," Max said. *The more you know about your enemy, the better*, he thought. "How do you know her?"

"I don't want to talk about her," Roger said. "She's a nasty piece of work, that's all I'll say."

Max and Lia shared a look. There was

clearly some history here that Roger didn't wish to share.

"Well, I agree, she seemed pretty nasty to me," Max said.

"Oh, you've had dealings with her, have you?" Roger asked. "Then you know what she's like."

"Yes – but she won't be able to fight and win against two whole fleets, will she?" Max said. "Not even with the Professor on her side. This time, she's bitten off more than she can chew!"

"I wouldn't be so sure, lad," Roger said, looking uneasy.

"You don't have to come with us," Lia said. With a sweep of her arm she gestured at the wide blue ocean. "You can go anywhere you like, we're not stopping you."

"I wouldn't desert me old shipmates!" Roger said. "Don't you worry about that.

I'm just saying, Cora Blackheart always has a nasty trick up her sleeve, that's all."

"I know, believe me," Max said. "She and the Professor built a clone of my mother to trick me. I wouldn't put anything past her."

"Shiver me timbers! A clone, eh?" Roger said. "Just the sort of devious plan she'd think of. What did your mum say about that, then?"

"I don't know," Max said. He suddenly felt a lump in his throat. "My mum's still missing. I don't even know if she's alive or dead!"

"Well, she must be alive if they made a clone of her," Roger said. "Because they'd have had to use her DNA, wouldn't they?"

Max's heart quickened, hope rushing through him. "Would they?" he asked.

"That's how I understand it, anyhow," Roger said. "A marine biologist once told me all about it in a bar."

"What's DNA?" Lia asked.

"Stuff in the cells of your body," Roger said. "It's like a code that makes you just the way you are."

"Do Merryn have it?" Lia asked.

"Every living thing has it," Roger said. "You, me, sponges, jellyfish. And Max's mum."

Max was silent. He was still trying to make sense of this news. His mother was alive very recently. Probably. And if so, she met the pirates. Perhaps they had captured her in order to carry out their plan? Realisation dawned on him. *It's possible the pirates are still holding her captive*, Max thought. *And she might even be imprisoned on the* Pride of Blackheart, *not far away*. He felt a steely determination, as strong as the vernium of his hyperblade. He was going to get her back.

Boots came clicking up behind them, and Max turned to see General Phero approaching. "Our ships are all in order. We are ready to depart and link up with the Aquoran fleet! If you wish, you may come on the Gustadian flagship with me."

"Thanks," said Max, "but I'll use my aquabike."

"Go on a ship?" Lia said, as if the idea was the most ridiculous thing she'd ever heard of. "What's wrong with swimming?"

"And I'll travel along with me old mates," Roger said. "I got me trusty rocket boots on." He leant down and slapped the heavy metal boots.

Max leaped onto his aquabike, followed by Rivet who clambered on behind. There were twin splashes as Lia and Roger dived into the sea.

Max looked ahead at the glinting blue ocean, with the ships of the Aquoran and Gustadian fleets dotted about. The Quest had

taken on a new meaning for him. They still
had one more chance to defeat the pirates
and save the cities of the Alliance. But they
also had to save Max's mother.

He twisted the throttle and his aquabike accelerated out into open water.

"All right, Cora," Max said under his breath. "Bring it on!"

Don't miss Max's next Sea Quest
adventure, when he faces

CHAKROL
THE OCEAN HAMMER

Sea Quest ®

Look out for all the books in
Sea Quest Series 4:

THE LOST LAGOON

REKKAR THE SCREECHING ORCA

TRAGG THE ICE BEAR

HORVOS THE HORROR BIRD

GUBBIX THE POISON FISH

OUT IN SEPTEMBER 2014!

Don't miss the
BRAND NEW
Special Bumper Edition:

SKALDA
THE SOUL STEALER

978 1 40832 851 4

OUT IN JUNE 2014

WIN AN EXCLUSIVE GOODY BAG

In every Sea Quest book the Sea Quest logo is hidden in one of the pictures. Find the logos in books 9-12, make a note of which pages they appear on and go online to enter the competition at

www.seaquestbooks.co.uk

Each month we will put all of the correct entries into a draw and select one winner to receive a special Sea Quest goody bag.

You can also send your entry on a postcard to:

Sea Quest Competition, Orchard Books,
338 Euston Road, London, NW1 3BH

Don't forget to include your name and address!

GOOD LUCK

Closing Date: May 31st 2014

DARE YOU DIVE IN?

www.seaquestbooks.co.uk

Deep in the water lurks a new breed of Beast.

Dive into the new Sea Quest website to play games,
download activities and wallpapers and read all
about Robobeasts, Max, Lia, the Professor
and much, much more.

Sign up to the newsletter at www.seaquestbooks.co.uk
to receive exclusive extra content, members-only
competitions and the most up-to-date
information about Sea Quest.

IF YOU LIKE SEA QUEST,
YOU'LL LOVE BEAST QUEST!

Series 1: COLLECT THEM ALL!

An evil wizard has enchanted the magical beasts of Avantia. Only a true hero can free the beasts and save the land. Is Tom the hero Avantia has been waiting for?

978 1 84616 483 5

978 1 84616 482 8

978 1 84616 484 2

978 1 84616 486 6

978 1 84616 485 9

978 1 84616 487 3

DON'T MISS THE
BRAND NEW SERIES OF:

Series 14: THE CURSED DRAGON

RAFFKOR
THE STAMPEDING BRUTE

978 1 40832 920 7

VISLAK
THE SLITHERING SERPENT

978 1 40832 921 4

TIKRON
THE JUNGLE MASTER

978 1 40832 922 1

FALRA
THE SNOW PHOENIX

978 1 40832 923 8

OUT NOW!

FINARIA
THE SAVAGE SEA SNAKE

Finaria is a powerful purple-and-green sea snake with yellow eyes. Metal spikes around its neck can be fired at enemies.

AGE	3
TECH POWER	169
COURAGE	95
FRIGHT FACTOR	91

GUSTADIANS

The Gustadian people have pale skin and jet-black oval eyes. They are remarkably strong and agile, and good with technology.

AGE	48
AQUA POWER	111
COURAGE	88
FRIGHT FACTOR	45

GLUE-GUN

The Gustadians are armed with weapons that shoot sticky strands which harden quickly and trap their victims.

AGE	3
TECH POWER	76
COURAGE	0
FRIGHT FACTOR	30

AQUORAN
BATTLE-CRUISER

Part of the Aquoran Defence Force, the speedy battle-cruiser is one of the ships that joins the battle against Cora Blackheart.

AGE	10
TECH POWER	113
COURAGE	0
FRIGHT FACTOR	41